Dear H

by

Diane Guntrip

15th July

Dear H,

I hate myself!! Do I shock you? You may think that's an awful thing to say, but it's true. I hate the way I look. I hate to look at myself in the mirror.

If you came to our house, you'd see beautifully framed photographs of my Mum, Veronica, when she was young. They are scattered about all over the place, in the hallway, on top of bookshelves, hanging on the wall. You can't escape from them. She's always smiling happily in these photographs. She had something to smile about.

When she was my age, she was tall, slim and

drop-dead gorgeous. She still is. Her long straight hair is as blonde and shiny as ever. It always seems to keep in perfect shape, even when it's windy. Her eyes, truly, are the colour of cornflowers and they are framed by the longest, thickest lashes. She doesn't even need to wear mascara. Wherever she goes, she makes an impact. People turn and stare in admiration, especially the men! I can't imagine any guy would ever look at me in that way when I'm older.

I'm not like her at all. I can't understand who I look like, certainly not like my tall willowy Mum or my super fit looking Dad. I don't seem to resemble either of my parents. I absolutely hate having my photograph taken. I hate looking in the mirror. I hate what I see. My face is round, pale and podgy, and it's covered with zits and freckles and I've got small, dark eyes that look like currants! And then there's my hair! Yuck!! I suppose the nearest description to a colour is copper, a bit like the colour of toffee, but it's dull and has a mind of its own. The problem is, it spirals out in all directions. Mum complained again this morning, "Amanda, you really must wash your hair every day. It looks like the back of a haystack!"

She's always moaning about something! If it's not my hair then it's my clothes, my room, my homework etc. I can't remember the last time she said anything good about me. I suppose when I do really look at my hair, which I try not to do very often, I have to agree with her. It is dull and greasy but every time I wash it, it springs out more than ever so I try not to wash it. I tie it back but straggly bits always seem to escape and it never looks great.

At last, now that I'm home, I can change out of my dreadful school uniform, which makes me look like a parcel tied up with string. I have to wear this disgusting, shapeless, washy-green shirt buttoned up to the neck. Then there's the brown and green striped tie which makes me feel as though I'm choking. I just haven't got the hang of tying it properly and so it always looks as though the knot is slipping and I get into trouble for being untidy. Added to this is a dark brown pleated skirt that has to cover the knees, except that mine seems to not only cover my knees, it's almost approaching my ankles. That's the problem with being so short and podgy. Then there's a brown blazer with the school badge emblazoned on the pocket, beige ankle socks, brown flat leather lace-up shoes and to top it all, in winter, there's a brown beret, again with the school badge on the front. I've left the worse item until last. I'm sure you'll laugh - it's a straw boater with ribbon encircling the brim in brown, green and gold stripes. This is part of the summer uniform. I ask you? It sucks!! Before I forget, it's compulsory for us to wear the head gear on our journey to and from school. If we are seen without it, we are given detention. I always feel such an idiot and can't wait to arrive home so I can change.

I've now changed into my favourite tee-shirt, the one with the glitter purple on the front. I always change into this shirt when I arrive home from school, although glitter purple isn't really me and I wouldn't be seen dead in it outside as it's too tight. The reason I wear it is because it reminds me of my favourite singing star. I've seen a photo of her wearing a similar one although she looks a 'million dollars' in hers. Mum bought it for me when

I was two sizes smaller. Before Mum arrives home, I cover my shirt with a big daggy old one so Mum can't see how ridiculous I look. I wear it with my track pants. At least they are comfy. Mum hates them and says, "You've got a wardrobe of beautiful clothes. Why do you have to wear those dreadful old pants and that hideous shirt?"

She obviously hasn't REALLY looked at me recently, otherwise she'd realise that all the clothes in my wardrobe are too small for me.

See yer,
Mandy

PS
I've just re-read what I've written. I can't believe it! Dear H........ it sounds as though I am writing to

a REAL PERSON! I think the 'H' should really stand for 'HELP' because I'm beginning to think that's what I need. I can't believe I've actually admitted it. I'm writing to someone WHO DOESN'T EVEN EXIST!! An imaginary friend at my age! I'd better keep this journal hidden otherwise people will think I'm going crazy! If Mum found out she'd be yanking me off to the nearest psyche.

When I received this journal and matching pen set, for a present from Gran, I hadn't a clue what I was going to use it for. It sat in my drawer carefully wrapped in tissue paper for a long while, and then, the idea came to me that I'd use it as a diary so I can write down all about my secret thoughts and feelings. I'm beginning to think writing to you H, would be fun. You could be the friend I've always wanted! Help!

1st August

Dear H,

Piggy, Piggy, Piggy!!! I can't get it out of my head! I hate it! "There you go again," I can hear you say!

Sorry, but I have to let off steam and I haven't anyone else to rant and rave to. Piggy is my nickname at school. There, I've admitted it. I've really had it up to here! When I stepped off the bus, coming home from school, the school bully, Cassandra, had to shout, "Bye Piggy! Fat bum! Bye Piggy!"

Even people walking along the street heard her and stared at me in a strange way as the bus raced off into the distance. I fixed my gaze on the pavement, pretended to ignore her and everyone else but deep down, I felt as if I wanted to crawl up into a tiny ball and roll away and never be seen again. Have you ever felt like that? I had to try really hard to stop the tears from escaping and rolling down my cheeks. I felt humiliated. It's not the first time she's done it, and I know it won't be the last.

Cassandra is ice-cold and calculating and she knows it gets to me and that's why she does it. She's always surrounded by her buddies and I can feel them smirking at me even if I'm not looking at them. When I walk into a classroom, they're always whispering and then they stop as soon as they see me and burst out laughing. I'd just love to get my own back but I don't know how I can on my own. I feel so isolated as if the whole world is against me. I'm going to start crying. I only do it when there's no one around and it's becoming a habit. I will look worse than ever!

I'm feeling a bit better now, even though I've got red circles around my eyes, my cheeks are blotchy and my nose is sore with all the blowing. I'd better splash it with cold water before Mum sees me.

St Ursula's College, which is the private girls' school I attend, is a nightmare from which I never escape. The fear hovers around me from when I wake up to when I go to bed. It's no better at the weekends. I never want to get out of bed, for as soon as I wake up, there is always something to remind me of school, like the homework, and when Sunday arrives, I spend all day worrying about Monday and what terrible things it will bring with it.

Mum insists I carry my mobile phone with me at all times. She says I need it for emergencies. If she only knew my life is a permanent emergency, but she isn't aware of that. Everyone at school has a mobile phone. They are always texting each other with stupid messages which they seem to find hilarious or they are sending really hurtful texts to me. I don't know how they got my number but the texts began to appear. Some of the things they say are really gross - too terrible for me to repeat even to you. I don't feel as though I have any peace from them as they never let up. As if that isn't enough, I've been sent threatening emails. I can't understand how they got my email address as I've never given it to them.

I got to the point where I couldn't stand it anymore. I felt as though I was a prisoner in my own home. It was bad enough with the offensive comments on the bus, but with all this other stuff - it's too hard. I've decided the only way to cope is for me to delete the emails without opening them and keep the phone switched off. I've felt so desperate; I've now hidden the phone in a case at the back of my walk-in-robe.

Mum keeps complaining that she can't contact me because my phone is always switched off. I have to keep making excuses. I would love to tell her why but I'm frightened. I'm scared of telling anyone, especially at school, as it's sure to cause a terrible fuss and then Cassandra and her buddies will make my life even more unbearable than it is already. I'm on the edge as it is. If only my favourite singer's lyrics were true,

'Upside down

Inside out,

The warmth of the sun

Will dry your tears,

And there'll be no more fears.'

Love,

Amanda

PS I've been thinking about phoning one of the
hotlines for kids to talk to one of their counsellors
about what is going on. I copied the number down
when I saw it flash onto the TV screen. Every
time I think about phoning the hotline, I get cold
feet and break out in a sweat. My heart starts
beating at twice its normal rate. It's not as
though it's just one problem and I wouldn't know
where to begin. Perhaps I'll phone another day.

1st September

Dear H,

I don't fit in with the majority of the girls at school, not the ones in my class anyway. All they seem to think about is how they appear to other people, whether they look cool, where they are going on holiday, which boys fancy them and the list goes on. I have to admit to you (but to no one else) that I haven't any friends, not one. How desperate does that make me sound?

One Sunday a short while ago, Mum decided to hold a fashion party at our house. Fashion is her life. Did I tell you that she owns a chain of boutiques? It was a charity event which included a three course lunch. A lot of the mothers of the girls from school decided that they would come and - horror of horrors - Cassandra's mother decided it would be a great idea if all of the mothers attended with their daughters. It's bad enough having to see the girls at school every day but having them altogether in our house on a Sunday, I can't think of anything worse. I tried thinking of all sorts of reasons why the girls couldn't come but Mum thought having the girls attend was the most marvellous idea. She couldn't understand why I didn't want the girls there and said, "Amanda, you are such a spoil sport."

Mum then decided that it would be a brilliant idea to include some teen fashions and asked Cassandra and her friends to be models. She really hurt me when she said, "It's a shame you can't be a model Amanda. Clothes always look better on slim girls."

I was really dreading the event. Mum made such a big thing of it. She was in her element arranging the lunch menus, the flowers, the music etc. A week before the event I was having daily migraines and by the time Sunday arrived, I had worked myself up into such a frenzy, I felt as though I would explode. I was so queasy with nerves that during the lunch I had to keep excusing myself and bolting off to the bathroom. Of course Mum kept commenting on it, "Goodness me, Amanda, can't you sit still for two minutes?"

That started everyone making their own snide comments whilst they nudged each other and tried not to giggle every time I stood up and excused myself. This made the situation worse than ever. My face became redder each time and I contemplated locking the bathroom door and staying there until everyone had left. I knew that would cause more of a fuss than ever, so I had no choice but to put on my brave face and try to laugh it off.

After lunch Mum suggested I take the girls upstairs and show them my room. I replied that I didn't think they'd be interested but, of course, they all wanted to see it. My room has always been decorated by the top interior designers in consultation with Mum and not particularly in the style I'd choose. I'd prefer my walls to be plastered with posters of my favourite vocalists, and all my stuffed toys scattered around.

Mum had to have a 'theme' for my bedroom design. She's mad on themes! So, I've ended up with a 'dream' theme with frills on everything possible, funky beaded lamps, sequined cushions in bright pinks and a mini dream catcher hanging from the bed post! It is very 'girly' and cool if you like that sort of thing, but I'm not that keen. Looking at me, you wouldn't describe me as 'girly' would you?

For once there wasn't anything there the girls could fault me on. You could see that they were impressed with the 'dream' theme by the envious expressions on their faces all except Cassandra who stuck her nose in the air, folded her arms, hunched her shoulders and began taking loud breaths that everyone could hear. She certainly did a good job of pretending to be bored. She's sure to discuss my room, pull it to pieces and convince all of the girls to be on her side and make my life even more miserable next week. Of course Mum had made sure that anyone going into any of the rooms in the house would be impressed. That's what is important to her.

By then, it was time for the fashion parade. Cassandra and the selected models slipped away to change into their tiny size 6 outfits. Cassandra couldn't help but make me feel more of a frump than ever, by announcing loudly in her crystal clear voice, "What a pity there isn't a dress small enough for you Amanda. You'd need elephant size!!"

Of course, everyone laughed even the adults. It's just not fair. It's an awful thing to say, but I don't believe anyone really likes me for who I am. No one really knows the real me hidden under all of this fat. I feel like an unborn baby. Everyone knows it's there but it's an unknown identity at this stage. I feel as though I want to be reborn. Don't laugh, I'm desperate to be the real me - all of you Pop Princesses, watch out!

From your 'frumpy fat friend'

Amanda

10th September

Dear H,

I spent all of recess and lunch time in the library today. I always sit in the corner and no one comes to sit near me. I'm not that horrible, am I? I spent most of the time with a book open on the table in front of me, a sheet of paper and a pencil. I had planned to begin my homework. I couldn't settle and my thoughts were racing in different directions. It didn't take long for them to drift back to the fashion parade and how, deep down inside, I would have loved to have been a model; I subconsciously began to doodle with my pencil on the spare sheet of paper in front of me.

My thoughts then turned to the unread texts
that I know will be waiting for me on my phone
if I ever check it. Even though I'm not reading
them, there is sure to be one about me being the
size of an elephant. I can't get these thoughts
out of my head. I'm scared.

When the bell rang for afternoon classes, I looked
down to pick up my things; I found I'd been
scribbling my thoughts down onto paper,

'Get out of my head!
Get out of my head!

You're in there with me
Causing distress.

I can't think straight,

I can't concentrate.

Get out of my head!

Get out of my head!'

From your 'frightened' friend,

Amanda

28th September

Dear H,

Another bad day!! Athletics!! We all have to train for Inter-School Competitions, whether we are selected or not. What a waste of time! This week everyone has to try out for long-jump and track events! All I do is pray for rain, hail, thunder and lightning - anything to call a halt to the practices. I would rather do anything than have to go out on the track, even French! Everyone else is so thrilled to escape from the classroom except me. No luck so far. The sun keeps a permanent vigil over the athletics track.

St Ursula's College prides itself on always winning! Its reputation, as a posh private school, seems to depend on us winning everything! Win! Win! Win! We are supposed to aim high in everything that we do. That's all we hear about. I don't get it! Sport is definitely not the most important thing in my life. Music and writing are far more important to me. How boring you say!

Last week I pretended to have an upset tummy so I could skive off from Sport. Ms Thomas, the Sports teacher, looked at me with her piercing stare and said in her loud clear voice that she uses on the track, "Not feeling well again Amanda!" and sent me off to see Matron in the Sick Bay.

Both Ms Thomas and Matron are becoming suspicious, as it's not the first time this has happened. The week before my excuse was that I was suffering from a raging migraine! The week before that I was genuinely sick. I'm beginning to run out of excuses. I can't have food poisoning every week and I haven't started my periods yet so I can't use that as an excuse!! Matron said firmly, "If you are unwell again Amanda, I will have to phone your mother."

That really worried me. For a start, I hate to be seen in my sports gear, a pale wishy-washy green top with the St Ursula's badge proudly displayed on the pocket, and you guessed it, brown shorts. I feel as though everyone is staring at me. My legs are so gross. They are so shapeless, pale, and freckly and they wobble when I run! I'm sure I've the beginnings of cellulite! My thighs are so lumpy! Do you know if girls of twelve get cellulite?

To make it worse, Cassandra has THE most perfect

legs. She's tall and skinny and, to make matters worse, she's really athletic. Ms Thomas seems to like her because she's good at sport. It's about the only thing she is good at!! She's represented the school in various track events and won, so the school is 'so proud' of her. She is also a 'cheerleader' and everyone in her clique is a cheerleader too! That means they are exclusive! They keep themselves to themselves and when they are together they are impossible. Cassandra seems to get away with anything and everything. You see, she is always SO polite to the teachers. They can't see anything wrong with her and wouldn't believe she could be so mean. If they read the texts I have received, they would get such a shock.

From 'Sporty' ha-ha!

Amanda

16th October

Dear H,

I've had a better day today! Or rather it began better!! I scored top marks in a French test! I did MY little bit to help the school WIN! I shouldn't be so sarcastic. I really did feel great.

At least it gave me a short break from Cassandra. She's not very good at French and was deliberately staring out of the window humming to herself as I went up to Madame to collect my test paper. That was an improvement. Her normal trick is to stick her feet out in the aisle between the desks in order to trip me up.

We had music today! It's my favourite lesson. I

would really like to audition for the school choir, as I love singing. I can't make up my mind whether to go for it or not. No one has ever told me that I have a good singing voice so I don't know whether I'll be accepted. The music teacher, Mr Brookes, auditions students to see if they are good enough. I'm a bit scared. I don't want to make a fool of myself. I'll think about it.

On the bus on the way home, Cassandra couldn't resist having a go at me again. She had all her so called friends crammed together with her in their usual places on the back seat and she said loudly, so that everyone on the bus could hear, "What a big head we have Piggy!"

"It's not as big as her bum!" shouted out one of her gang.

All her friends exploded with laughter - except for me. I could feel my blood beginning to boil. I was so fed up with being undermined. Because I'd beaten her in French, and knew she was hopeless at it, I suddenly found the confidence, for the first time, to get my own back. As I stood up to get off the bus, I looked at her and said in French, "Que tu as une Grande gueule!"

The whole bus applauded. As I stepped off the bus, I heard one of her friends explaining to her what I had said. I somehow don't think she'll be very pleased to hear she has a 'big mouth'. It felt so good at the time but when I began to walk away from the bus-stop, I began to shake when I realised what I'd done. I know you'll think that's stupid. You see, I should have kept my mouth closed. She'll make my life worse than ever now.

Yummy!!!

Yummy!!!

I've been home now for over an hour and Sylvia,
our home help, has left a note on the table saying
she's had to leave early so no one's in. I took the
opportunity of the house being empty and I headed
straight towards the pantry, raided it and have just
demolished a whole variety pack of chips, three Mars
Bars and a large bottle of lemonade! It has certainly
stopped me from shaking and taken my mind off the
incident on the bus. Eating makes me feel better and
gives me a buzz. I'm feeling better at the moment.
I know I shouldn't stuff myself because it will only
make me fatter, but I can't help myself.

One hour later and I'm not feeling so good. In
fact, I feel decidedly sick. Yuck! I'm asking myself,
"Why did I do it? Why? Why? Why?"

I'll never lose weight and look good. I'm so annoyed with myself. I feel so guilty. Every time I binge, I know that I'll feel like this later. Something upsets me and off I go and stuff myself. Do you do this when you are upset? You see programs about it on the TV and it's written about in Teen magazines but I've never heard about anyone actually talking about it.

I honestly can't stop stuffing myself with food, usually junk food. Afterwards I hate myself for doing it! I do! I do! I do! Is my life always going to be like this? It's as though I'm on a merry-go-round which goes round and round and I can't get off.

I've just used up half a box of tissues. When Mum arrived home from work, I looked such a wreck;

I told her I thought I was going down with the flu. Perhaps she'll let me stay off from school. That would be cool. It's all too complicated and I wouldn't know where or how to begin talking to her about how I feel. Anyway, she's far too busy to listen.

I don't know what I would do if I couldn't talk to you.

Your best friend,

Amanda

16th November

Dear H,

Mum's taken pity on me. She thinks I've got the 'flu. My acting skills must be improving. She's told me to have a day in bed and to phone her at her office if I feel worse. If I'm not feeling better by tomorrow, she says she'll make a doctor's appointment for me. I had better make a quick recovery!! I do not want to be dragged off to the doctor again. The last time I visited him, he droned on and on about my weight. He made me feel ten times worse and then to make matters worse, Mum started to moan at me and told me how much better I would look and feel if I were slimmer. Just what I needed to hear when I know it's true.

I've been day-dreaming on and off throughout the day. Memories from the past have been floating around in my head. I'll try to put them in order for you. When I was little, Mum didn't work and was always at home. I was her pride and joy. She used to cuddle me and tell me how pretty I was. She spent lots of time with me, took me out and showed me off to her friends. I can remember when I was small and we attended family parties, I was always asked to stand up and sing in front of everyone. They used to clap, and say how clever I was and tell me what a lovely voice I had. It made me feel so warm inside.

How things have changed! Before Mum married Dad she had graduated from Uni with a Degree in Business Studies. When I was five, and began attending school full-time, Mum opened her first boutique, selling designer clothes. Mum has a lot of wealthy friends and they began to buy from the boutique, and it became an overnight success and definitely THE place to shop.

As the business developed, Mum became more ambitious. She wasn't happy with one boutique. She had to have more. She now runs a chain of boutiques; all called 'Veronica K'. You will find branches in the major cities and they are all she seems to think about. Her main topic of conversation revolves around sales targets and the possibility of expanding overseas. Don't get me wrong. I'm proud of her. She's done extremely well in a short space of time. She's won Business Awards, has been featured in top fashion magazines and is always seen in the social pages of the newspapers where she is always described as being 'successful, elegant and charming'.

She doesn't seem to understand or even think about why I'm so different from her. All she does is moan about me, Amanda the Friendless Fashion Victim!! She's so cool. She's a perfectionist. I must be a great disappointment to her. I feel a failure. Some days I feel so depressed that I don't want to get up, even though the sky is blue and I have every material thing I could want, there's this cavernous hole inside me, so deep, that nothing will fill it. Perhaps it's time I should make the effort to phone the hotline for kids.

I think Mum has given up on me. She usually arrives home late after the boutiques have closed. She frequently travels all over the country on business trips and quite often overseas, where she attends fashion shows or buyers' meetings. I'm sure that when she's at work, and she becomes so engrossed in all the facets of the fashion industry, she forgets all about me. Even though she asked me to call her if I felt worse, I'm not expecting her to call me to ask me if I'm okay. It would make my day if she did! Thankfully, when she does phone, she calls me on the landline when she expects me to be home.

Mum just doesn't appear interested in me now that I'm no longer cute. Sometimes when she's had a hard day, she's so short tempered and says some really hurtful things. Can't she see that I'm still the same person inside that I was when I was small?

I'm thinking of some song lyrics I've heard recently on the radio which really sum up how I feel,

'Many harsh words have been spoken,

Cruel thoughts have been revealed.

You tell me to act my age.

Listen to how I feel.'

From

'Daydreamer' Amanda

3rd December

Dear H,

I've been feeling guilty since I spoke to you last time. I feel rather ashamed of the way in which I've described my mother to you. She can, and has been mean to me on occasions. She doesn't always show me the love I crave but then I'm not perhaps the perfect daughter she would like to have. I was feeling so utterly dejected, as well as being terrified of what Cassandra would do next. When I'm like that, nothing in my life is right.

At times, Mum really has made an effort to help me. She did take me to visit a weight-loss counsellor and she did join me on a diet, even though she didn't need to lose weight. She was the one who lost the weight and I didn't lose any weight at all, in fact, I put weight on. She was really disappointed and I felt as though I had let her down, so she gave up on that. I really wanted to lose the weight and I followed their diet, but when things at school got tough, and Cassandra and her clique got to me, I couldn't help myself.

I would get off the bus earlier than normal and call in at the super-market. There I bought all kinds of junk food and I would cross the road and find a wooden bench in a secluded spot in Jarvis Park. I would sit huddled up and hope that no one would recognise me in my school uniform.

After I had stuffed myself, I would throw all the wrappings in a rubbish bin and then walk home. Sylvia never seemed to make any comment even if she did notice I was a bit late. I'm not proud of myself. In fact I feel ashamed and guilty and I never want Mum to find out. She would be livid!

She also suggested that I join some clubs after school, but most of them are sport related, and you know how I feel about sport. That was a huge 'No' from the start. Mum also suggested I attend a youth camp. It was supposed to help with my self-esteem and was run by a local church during the school holiday. I said I would give the idea some thought but I couldn't face going. I would have had to have slept in a shared dormitory with other girls and shared a bathroom. I couldn't face that with everyone poking fun at how I looked in my PJs.

I haven't mentioned my Dad, have I? He's a senior partner in a commercial law firm in the city. I don't see much of him either because he has to work long hours, especially when they are preparing for a case. Sometimes he doesn't arrive home until the early hours of the morning when I'm in bed. I think he thinks everything is just fine. He has no idea how bad things really are. He tends to bury his head in the sand when it comes to anything to do with 'women' and he imagines that everything between Mum and his daughter is cool. I don't think he's really looked at me for ages. He either has his head hidden behind a newspaper or is locked away in his study when he's not at the office.

He hasn't always been like that. He used to idolise me when I was younger, just as Mum did. We've all drifted apart. Mum and Dad do get on fine when they see each other but all they talk about is their work. I suppose in some ways we could be called a dysfunctional family. I think that's the word I'm thinking of. Isn't it awful? It's worse than awful, it's really lame!

Don't get me wrong, I'm not on my own all the time. When I arrive home from school there's often someone in the house. Mum uses the local home help agency, 'Angels'. Sylvia, who I have mentioned before, is from the agency. She's been with us ever since we moved into this house. She's okay and Mum seems pleased with her but she doesn't have much time to talk to me. She seems to have enough problems with her own family. I hear about them but she rarely asks me how I am. There always seems to be a crisis of some kind or another in her life. As soon as she's finished working at our house, off she goes to baby-sit one of her many grandchildren. There is always someone in her family who has to go to work in the evening and needs Sylvia to help out.

Sylvia supervises the general day to day running of the house which is huge, six bedrooms each with an ensuite bathroom, kitchen, family room, lounge room, dining room, games room, home theatre, conservatory and so the list goes on. Why we need such a big house to rattle around in when there are only the three of us, I don't know. Some of the rooms are only used when Mum and Dad entertain and they are so busy working, that doesn't happen very often. Sylvia spends all day keeping everything spick and span and prepares dinner so that Mum, or whoever is in can heat it up. She usually leaves the house not long after I arrive home.

Mum sometimes phones me after school, if she has the time, to check that I'm okay. It's really a 'duty' call. If she's too busy, she'll ask her secretary to phone instead. Occasionally, we'll have a chat and I feel we're getting somewhere. Mainly, she's abrupt and you can tell she's got other things on her mind.

When I arrive home from school and Sylvia is nowhere in sight, I head straight for the kitchen to pick out a snack, or should I say snacks, and retreat to my room. I sit stuffing myself until it's time for dinner, which I usually eat by myself if Mum and Dad aren't home. Then I'll do my homework, and then I might play some CDs. That's my favourite thing of all. If no one can hear me I'll sing along with the music. It really helps when you concentrate on the words and what they mean. But that's my secret. Promise you'll not tell a soul?

I pretend to be my favourite vocalist. She's awesome! She's an incredible performer and her shows are out of this world. I wish I had a voice as good as hers and looked as cool as she does! I love the words from her song,

'You have youth,

You have beauty,

You have talent,

You have wealth,

But inside are you happy?

Are you free from hurt and pain?'

I read where she became famous when she won a talent show on TV. Part of the prize was the chance to record a CD. I would love to have the chance to do that but who am I kidding? I haven't even got the confidence to audition for the school choir.

Feeling nervous,

Amanda

6th January

Dear H,

I bet you think I do nothing else but moan, moan, moan! It's half way through the school holiday. We've had Christmas and New Year. Now it's like it never happened. Mum was so busy with the boutiques before Christmas; she actually paid to have someone come in to the house to put up all the Christmas decorations.......would you believe it? I did offer to help but she said if I did them nothing would match!! I'm not a complete idiot! Remember her themes? Well, this year it was Switzerland! Thankfully, she stopped at us all wearing Swiss National Costume but she did insist on having fake snow! I must admit it did look pretty. Not that poor Sylvia appreciated it as she was the one who had the job of removing it. It seemed to stick everywhere and to everything. Somehow, I don't think we'll be having it again, not if Sylvia has her way.

Straight after Christmas there were the January Sales to prepare for so, of course, Mum had to take control of that. Dad took two weeks off from work. He wasn't pleased with Mum about her going into the office for the preparation for the sales and told her she'd have to learn to delegate! That will be the day! She thinks that she's the only one who can do her job properly.

I suppose Christmas wasn't too bad. We spent most of the holiday visiting Mum and Dad's friends. All of our close family live far away from us. Mum did apologise to me and admitted it wasn't the ideal situation. Well, to be honest, it was boring. Most of their friends haven't children of my age. When they saw me they nearly all said, "Happy Christmas Amanda. My, haven't you grown!"

Thankfully, they were too polite to mention that I'd grown outwards rather than upwards!
They soon forgot about me as the conversation centred on their work. No one thought to include me and as I sat there in silence they commented on how quiet I was. I felt like screaming at them. What do they expect if they talk about work all the time? On the way home Mum said, "Do you always have to look so miserable Amanda? Surely you can smile and be polite? You are so fortunate. We give you everything and you just don't appreciate it do you?"

The words from a song I'd scribbled down came
into my head,

'I'm crying in my heart
With every song I sing.
Everyone believes
I've everything.'

I just started writing a few of my feelings down on
paper. I think it helps. When I'm in the shower, I
make up my own tune to the words. Hope no one
ever hears me!! Mum and Dad just have no idea of how
I really feel. I'm twelve, not twenty five! If I confided
in them they would say, "What's your problem?"

When I think about it, I suppose I don't really
have anything to complain about compared to
some people. Most girls would jump at the chance

to live in a house like I do. Mum and Dad are wealthy. There's a swimming pool, sauna and tennis court. I have my own interior designed bedroom, adjoining lounge room and bathroom but I'm not happy. I look around and ask myself, "What's wrong with me?"

My parents pay for me to attend a prestigious school, even though I hate the place. I could have anything I wanted and yet there's something missing. There's a great big hole inside of me that never seems to be filled. Sometimes it's bigger than at other times. I'm in a deep dark pit and I can't climb out of it. Sometimes I feel that I can cope better than at other times, but the feeling is always with me to some extent. I don't know what to do. I'm still thinking about phoning the hotline for kids but it's a big step.

'I don't know why I feel this way.

Sometimes, I don't know how to feel at all.

Will there ever come a day

To lift the dark clouds right away?'

This sounds SO depressing! Soon, you'll begin to give up on me. I've not always felt like this. I can remember feeling happy but it was such a long time ago. I didn't feel like this when Mum was at home. It's not that I want her to stop working. I just need to feel wanted and important, to be recognised for who I am.

When I was small, she seemed so different and lots of fun. I can remember her making up silly songs and we would giggle like mad at stupid things. Mum was always goofing around and cracking corny jokes. She always had time to talk to me and take me out. Even though Dad was working hard then to become a successful lawyer, he always had Sunday off from work. We always went out as a family. Dad used to say it was his "weekly date with his two gorgeous girls." That was before we moved into this house. Everything seems to have gone wrong since then. Mum and Dad seem so wrapped up in their own lives that they don't seem to have time for me and it hurts. All I want is their love and approval. I sometimes think they would be better off without me.

I wish I could talk to my parents about how I feel. They have absolutely no idea. They would get such a shock if they knew what was going on in my head. They think, because I've got everything I should be the happiest girl around. I can't talk to them. I just can't. They have no idea about how

I feel. They would think I'm so ungrateful and I'm not. I must try to pull myself together but it's such a struggle and I just have no idea of how or where to begin. Think I'll check up on the hotline number again.

I don't know what I would do if I couldn't spend time writing to you. H, you are a legend! You are heaps better than a real friend as you just listen and that's what I need. You don't try to tell me what I should do. Thank you for listening to me. I really will try to be more cheerful next time.

From a 'depressed' Amanda

1st February

Dear H,

The holidays are over and I've returned to the
'dungeon'. I think that is what I will call school
from now on.

Hurray! Sport is cancelled this week. That is terrific
news for me! Cassandra wasn't too happy. Sport
is the only thing she excels at. She's still the same.
I've noticed that she only looks happy when
she and her buddies are being mean to someone.
She'll walk around with her head held high with a
smirk written across her face. When you see her,
you know she's in the plotting stage and that
something awful is going to happen.

Cassandra's gang always appear as though they are all joined together at the hip by glue. You never see them alone. I've heard that Cassandra makes all the members of her clique stick to HER rules. She is so intimidating. That's why they all sit on the same seats everyday on the bus and they always eat their lunch together on the same bench at school. Heaven help anyone else who would dare to sit there.

Did I tell you that our class has been invited to the dress rehearsal of a concert that is being held at Cranfield High, a neighbouring school? It's in the afternoon so we miss all of our lessons. Great! Can't wait!

I've heard the school choir rehearsing a new song. I keep singing it over and over. I think I know all the words backwards. I wish I could sing really well but who would want to listen to me? I've still not decided whether to try out for the school choir. One day I have the confidence and then something bad happens and I tell myself that I'm being stupid and that I'm no good at anything. I think I'm afraid of being turned down and everyone knowing about it. Cassandra wouldn't leave me in peace.

Mum unexpectedly came home with a migraine early the other afternoon and I was singing one of my favourite songs at the top of my voice,

'You only have one chance
At this game we call life.
You can't come back a second time
So make sure you get it right.'

She said, "What a miserable song! If you keep singing as loud as that, you'll ruin your voice!"

I don't seem to be able to do anything to please her.

I don't think I'm ever going to sing again!

Amanda

10th February

Dear H,

Wow! My emotions are running riot! It must be the dreaded hormones. One minute I'm up on a rollercoaster high in the sky with not a care in the world and next I'm crashing down to earth, too tired to crawl out of the hole. Do you ever feel like that?

I don't know where to begin! Well, I'll start with the concert. It was just awesome. You know how I said I was never going to sing again? Well I just don't think I can stop myself. The need is almost as strong as eating and you know I'm an expert at that!

Let me tell you about the concert. We arrived and sat in the school theatre. Deep down in a secret part of my heart, I felt as though I wished I could have been taking part. I wished I could have been on the stage singing.

What a stupid thing to say! I can't even face auditioning for the school choir let alone thinking I could go up on stage and sing.

Well, the concert began. I enjoyed it so much and became so engrossed in it that for a while I forgot all about my problems. Most of the items in the first half of the concert were instrumental. I noticed that for the last act before the interval, someone had come onto the stage to lower the microphone. The audience was cheering loudly and when the curtains swished back I was surprised to see a girl sitting in a wheelchair on the stage. She was very pretty with long dark hair. I thought the audience was cheering loudly to be kind to the girl and, at first; I didn't take too much notice of her. The girl announced the songs she was about to sing and the school orchestra began to play. She was incredible! Her voice was like nothing I've heard before! It was strong and deep with a raw feeling to it and it was as though the girl was singing straight from her heart. I didn't notice the wheelchair. I was so entranced by the beauty of her voice. The atmosphere in the theatre was electric. I wouldn't have missed it for the entire world.

When she had finished, the audience stood up and cheered for more. The girl looked so radiantly happy. I know it may sound stupid but at that moment I actually envied her. Eventually, the curtains swished into closed position and the girls walked out for drinks. I suddenly realised that I was left sitting there on my own, glued to the seat, and that I had tears streaming down my face. I felt so embarrassed and hoped no one had noticed. I think they were all too busy chatting. I hope so.

As I left the theatre I couldn't describe to you how I felt. I was 'up-in-the-air'; almost weightless as if I could fly. When everything had settled down I began to feel a strange kind of excitement bubbling away under the surface. It's a strange feeling, really weird. I can't remember feeling like it for ages.

Flying high!

Love, Amanda

13th February

Dear H,

You really must promise me that you won't tell a single soul. Promise me? Ever since I came home from the concert I haven't been able to stop thinking about the girl in the wheelchair. It's as though my brain has been on auto pilot, with a will of its own. I've had no control over my thoughts. They've been whirling around so much I've been tossing and turning all night and have hardly slept a wink. I feel absolutely drained.

If the girl in the wheel chair can go on the stage and sing, why can't I? She's got heaps more problems than I have. One minute I think it could actually happen. That's the ME inside talking. Then the next minute the Amanda, that everyone makes fun of, steps in and tells me to stop being such an idiot. I know I'm fat and I'll have to lose weight. I feel so alone and unsure of myself. I wish I had lots of friends to support me. I would be the laughing stock of the school if anyone knew what was going off in my head. I feel that there is this little me inside of this big body. The fatter I've become the more of the real Amanda has disappeared.

Why is life so hard? I've decided not to tell anyone about this except for you.

Trying to escape,

Yours, Amanda

17th February

Dear H,

Help! I'm freaking out! It's hopeless. I can't do it!! I don't even know why I thought I could! I wouldn't know where to begin. You must think I'm stupid! Why did I ever think I could change myself? No one takes any notice of me. They all think I'm a 'nobody' and that my feelings don't matter.

I wish I could be myself and that everyone knew the REAL me.

Do you know, I've never told anyone, except for you, that I want to be a singer? I can't see it ever happening. It's really such a stupid idea. I will have to try and be more like the girl in the wheel

chair. The words from the song she sang at the
concert haunted me,

'Life is meant for living,
Not for moping away
Over chances never taken
For regrets will always stay.'

The girl hadn't let her problem affect her. She was
certainly living. If only I really felt that way.

From a 'confused' Amanda

23rd February

Dear H,

Thank you! Just talking it out to you helps me to put things in order. I don't know what I would do without you. I feel much calmer; more at peace. You are the only person who really knows me. Everyone else just thinks I'm a blob. If they thought I wanted to go on a stage and sing they would make my life a misery. I would be called every name Cassandra and her buddies could think of. Cassandra would wet herself laughing. When I write to you I always feel that everything is possible,

'Don't waste or spoil your gifts.

Don't throw your life away.

Have strength in your own convictions.

Make that promise to yourself today.'

Cheers, living in hope, Amanda

28th February

Dear H,

I feel really guilty about envying the singer in the wheelchair. I overheard Cassandra talking at school. She always talks so loudly that you can't help but hear what she has to say. She was telling one of her friends that the girl in the wheelchair, who sang at the concert, had been in a horse riding accident. She's now a paraplegic and will never be able to walk again. That is dreadful. I feel really sad. I couldn't begin to imagine what life must be like for her.

I have SO MUCH to be thankful for, and as Mum said at Christmas, I really don't appreciate it.

From a 'guilty' Amanda

3rd March

Dear H,

Sometimes it's great being on my own as you can do stuff and no one knows a thing about it! I've been standing in front of the mirror in my room imagining I'm up on stage. It's the only time I feel confident when I'm in my room on my own. I put one of my CDs on and sang every song at the top of my voice,

'I'll not give up
I'll not give in
I'll puzzle it out
And somehow I'll win.'

I was so engrossed singing along that I nearly missed the phone call. I didn't rush to answer the phone as hardly anyone, except Mum ever phones me at home and she had already rung me.

This time, I got a surprise as the call was for me. It was a long distance call from my Gran. I don't see her that often because she lives on the east coast, the other side of the country from us and Mum and Gran don't really seem to hit it off. It's a shame as I've always wished I could spend more time with Gran. She's not like Mum at all. At first I thought she wanted to speak to Mum but she said it was me she wanted to talk to. I had a chat with her, although she did most of the talking. She finished the conversation by saying, "As it's your 13th birthday in a couple of months, dear, I wondered if there was anything special you would like as a gift from me? Think about it and let me

know."

Perhaps I should phone Gran more often.

From a 'reflective' Amanda

11th March

Dear H,

I didn't think of the idea straight away. At first it was only a tiny bubble. I've been thinking ever since the concert how marvellous it would be to be able to sing properly. When it comes to my school work, I usually try to do my best so why shouldn't I do the same with my singing even if it's only for my own enjoyment. The more I've thought about it, the bigger the bubble has grown. It's almost ready to burst!

I'm still filled with doubts. You see, I think I'd like to have singing lessons!! Well, at least give them a go. It's hard to think positively when I feel I've got so much stacked against me. I feel so afraid because of what people will think of me. I don't suppose it should matter what anyone thinks, but it does.

I'm even nervous about asking Gran to pay. You see, I've decided to ask her if she will pay for some singing lessons for me!! I'd like that to be my 13th birthday gift!

Wish me luck!

Amanda

18th March

Dear H,

Well, I plucked up my courage and I phoned Gran yesterday before Mum arrived home. I think Gran was surprised. She said, "Are you sure that's what you want?"

I hope I sounded convincing even though I had to swallow hard before I replied hurriedly, "Yes please. That's what I want more than anything."

"Well, if you are certain, I'll see what I can do," she said.

I'm sure she thought there was something wrong with me because she kept asking me if I was okay.

She seemed even more surprised when I begged her not to tell Mum what I'd asked for.

From your 'giddy' friend,

Mandy

23rd March

Dear H,

I keep thinking about the singing lessons. I've been asking myself, "Am I doing the right thing?" Gran seemed a bit surprised when I asked her for them. Perhaps she thinks it would be a waste of time and money.

Part of me says, "Yes," and another part says, "Don't be so stupid!"

"I think we've had this conversation before," I hear you say!

You'll never guess? Gran's phoned again. We had quite a long chat. You'll never believe it? She told

me how, when she had been young, she had wanted
to be an actress. When she had mentioned this to
her father (my great Grandad) he had turned blue
in the face. He had shouted, "No daughter of mine
is going to go on the stage!"

Gran explained that when she was young you didn't
disobey your parents and the subject was never
referred to again. She said that she had never
forgotten the incident and had never stopped
wanting to go on the stage. She waited until she
was grown up and could make her own decisions
before she followed her aspirations. As an adult,
she'd been involved in amateur dramatics and
had starred in a few productions. She told me
she knew a few people in the 'business.' These
people, who had once been amateurs, had worked
their way up to being professional. I found it all

fascinating. Mum had never mentioned any of this to me.

It's strange how you never really know a person. I would never have thought in a million years that Gran would have wanted to become an actress when she was younger. I value her honesty and I feel privileged and special that she confided in me. It got me thinking about other people's lives. I wonder how many people have secrets that they keep hidden away and never share with anyone. I'm beginning to think that perhaps we never really know a person fully. I'm so glad that I've got you because I can tell you everything and you always accept me the way I am. You always listen to me and never tell me what I should do.

From your 'grateful' friend, Amanda

30th March

Dear H,

If you were a real person, instead of someone in my mind, I would begin this letter by asking you, "How are you doing?"

Anyone reading these letters must think I'm selfish and that I'm not in the least bit interested in anyone else. That's not true at all. I just have to off-load. All these thoughts are continually whirling around in my mind. To talk them out is my way of dealing with them. It keeps me sane. Just be thankful you aren't real. You'd get really sick of listening to all of my problems.

I don't know why I never thought of phoning

Gran for a chat before. She's so easy to talk to and she tells me lots of things about when Mum was young. It's as though I'm learning to know my Mum through Gran's eyes. I'm finding out all kinds of things about her. I didn't know Mum had been interested in going on the stage. Reading between the lines, I'm getting the idea that perhaps Mum wasn't that fantastic at it!!! Gran's good fun too. She makes me laugh.

Mum usually talks to Gran on the phone once a week. I get the impression she only phones her because she feels she has to and not because she wants to. I know Gran would like to become closer to Mum because she's told me. Their relationship hasn't always been like this. I hope it'll improve as I think Gran is really lonely since Pa died, but she won't admit it.

Gran has promised not to tell Mum about our secret. At first she thought it was rather strange that I hadn't asked Mum and Dad if I could have singing lessons. It's not as though they couldn't afford them. I made up the excuse that I wanted to surprise them.

She told me she was doing some research and trying to find a local singing teacher for me, someone who has a good reputation. She's contacting some people she used to know in the theatre. We've decided that if I attend the lessons straight after school, Mum and Dad won't know anything about what I'm doing. If I get caught, I can always tell a white lie and say I'm going round to a friend's place or I had to stay later at school. They wouldn't have any idea whether I've got friends or not.

Gran says she will post a small gift to me for my birthday so no one will be suspicious. Not that they'd notice.

From a 'sneaky' Amanda

8th April

Dear H,

It's only four weeks to my 13th birthday. Mum's been asking me for ages if I'd like a party. I'm not blown away with the idea. Mum's idea of a party and mine are different. She'd like me to invite hoards of friends and particularly suggested I invite 'my lovely friend Cassandra!' She began mentioning Themes! Fairy lights in the garden! A band and caterers!!! HELP!! She said, "You're only 13 once. If you don't have a party, you'll look back when you are older and regret it."

I don't think so. I've got a 'slight' problem in that, at the most, I could only invite around six girls and then I don't know whether they'd come. I couldn't call them friends. As I go to an all girls' school,

I hardly know any boys. I can't invite complete

strangers. It's not going to be much of a 'rave-

up' with six. Mum said, "I've been asking you

for weeks if you wanted to have a party. If we

leave it any longer, it will be too late to organise

anything."

Perhaps Gran can help me think of some way to

get out of it. I hope so.

Wish me luck,

Amanda

15th April

Dear H,

Thanks for Gran!! She's a legend!! I rang her and told her what Mum had in mind for my birthday. I told her I just couldn't face it. Guess what? I'm so excited! I'm going to spend my 13th birthday with Gran! Mum thought it was very odd and kept going ON and ON and ON about it. "Why on earth do you want to go all that way and spend your birthday with an old lady when you could have a super party?" she asked.

I muttered my way around it and said I hadn't seen Gran for a long while and the flight would be fun and it would be exciting to spend some time in another city etc. Phew!! Mum finally gave in and booked a flight for me. She even arranged for me to leave school early at lunch time so I could catch the flight and arrive early in the evening.

It's really great that my birthday falls on a Saturday so I can spend the weekend away. It will be awesome!!

From an 'excited' Amanda

11th May

Dear H,

Well, unfortunately, the good times don't last forever and I'm now home again. I can't say I'm chuffed about it. I wish I could have stayed for longer. I have so much to write about. I had THE most marvellous birthday!! I just wish I had a real friend to share all my news with.

Gran is really cool. I arrived early on Friday evening after a five and a half hour flight. Gran met me at the airport. I hadn't seen her for so long that I wondered if I'd recognise her but I needn't have worried. She is the most amazing person. She's really trendy and doesn't appear old at all! She told me she was sixty-six last birthday. I couldn't believe it. She's very slim with all the curves in the right places. I wish I had a figure like that! She has short hair which is coloured with an auburn tint and she was wearing a small amount of make-up. The one thing that really stands out is her eyes. They are beautiful and framed still with the most amazingly long eyelashes. She was dressed in a top designer pair of jeans and a fitted jacket. She greeted me with a warm hug. I could immediately see a resemblance to Mum. It's obvious where Mum has learnt her love of fashion.

When we arrived at her home, even though it was late, we sat and talked for ages. There were lots of things I thought I'd never share with anyone but I felt I could relate to her. Before long, I found myself opening up and I ended up blabbing about how I feel about lots of stuff, home, school,

Cassandra and her mean buddies, my weight and how I wish I had more friends etc. Gran just sat and listened, just like you do.

Before I went to bed, Gran asked, "Is there anything special that you would like to do tomorrow?"

"Can I sleep on it and let you know in the morning? I'm just so tired I can't think straight."

"Of course you can. Off you go to bed." she replied.

I went to bed and lay there thinking about what I'd like to do for my birthday and before I knew it, it was light, the sun was streaming through the window and it was MY BIRTHDAY!

After Grandpa died, Gran decided to move into an apartment so she wouldn't have to look after a large garden. We had breakfast on the balcony as it was warm weather. From there you can see the bay. It's just awesome! I opened my cards. Mum had packed a gift from her and Dad. Guess what? It was a new mobile phone (pink, of course!) which does everything possible!! My heart skipped a beat when I saw it. Then I thought that perhaps it wasn't such a bad gift. This phone would have a different number to my other one. I just had to make sure that Cassandra never found out what the number was and occasionally give Mum the impression that I was using it.

I tried hard to concentrate on my birthday and not let the thoughts of Cassandra's frequent texts hurt me. That would mean she had won. I wasn't going to let that happen. No way am I going to let Cassandra spoil my birthday.

Gran said she was keeping her special birthday surprise for me until that evening but she gave me a small gift to open at the breakfast table. It was a selection of small perfumes and teen make-up. She said, "I'll help you to put on some make-up this evening. The idea is to wear make-up so that no-one knows you're wearing it."

As I couldn't decide what I wanted to do, and I had arrived so late the night before, Gran suggested we book on a Shuttle Tour of the city. She said it would last for about five hours and would take in the major sights. It also meant that we wouldn't overtire ourselves for the evening as we'd be sitting down for part of the trip. We had a fantastic time being driven around the city, hopping off to look at the famous parks, museums and the cathedral as well as treating ourselves to a light seafood lunch and having a look in some of the shops. Gran suggested we visit one in particular where she treated me to a new dress for the evening surprise. She made no mention of my size and neither did the assistant for which I was thankful. I did wonder whether she'd set this up as the dress was perfect for me. You may think that would be boring for someone my age but I thoroughly enjoyed sharing it all with Gran.

One thing I really like about Gran is that she doesn't put pressure on me. She made no comments about how I looked. With Gran's help I forgot I was a frump and just enjoyed myself.

Okay, Gran did look a million dollars, but the way she treated me was more of an equal. Instead of the decisions being made for me, she actually discussed the day with me and it made such a difference.

We returned to the apartment around 5pm as Gran said, "As we are going out on the town, we ought to start thinking of getting ready. When you've had a shower and are dressed, come into my bedroom and I'll put your hair up for you and show you how to use some of that make-up."

She's amazing! With just the aid of an elastic band, a brush and the addition of some pins, it was up! I could never do it like that. She helped me put on a little of the make-up that she had given me and with a spray of the perfume we were ready to go. I felt like a princess for the first time since I was a little girl. I still didn't know where I was going. It was VERY exciting! Gran had arranged for a chauffer driven car to collect us and we were driven to a restaurant with city views!! I kept thinking, "I wish Cassandra could see me now!"

From our seats in the restaurant you could see the bay with all the different coloured lights from the buildings illuminated on the water. I felt so special. The waiters seemed to know it was my birthday. (I wonder how??) When it came time for dessert, a huge chocolate mud cake was brought in which had sparklers alight on top. Three of the waiters, one with a guitar, appeared from nowhere. The waiter with the guitar began to play Happy Birthday and the other two joined in singing. Everyone in the restaurant turned to look at me and some actually joined in with the singing! It was the first time since I'd arrived at Gran's that I'd felt embarrassed. She said, "I'm going to forget all about my diet tonight, Amanda. It's a very special occasion. Come on 'dig in'. I'm going to!"

When the cake was cut, everyone cheered and I felt as though everyone was on my side for a change. She then gave me an envelope and told me to open it. Inside was a business card with a name, Holly Field, an address, not far off from where I live, and phone details. Underneath those there was a long list of letters indicating the lady's qualifications, although at the time I didn't know what they meant. I was speechless. Gran said, "Don't look so surprised. Isn't that what you wanted for a gift?"

"Yes, oh yes. Thank you so much. It's just that I am so pleased but I also feel nervous as well," I managed to stutter.

"Well, I don't think you need to be nervous at all. I heard you singing in the shower and I think you'll do fine. Anyway, it's time for us to leave. The chauffeur is outside waiting to whisk us off."

When I asked her where to, she replied, "Wait and see. Come on."

I will never forget my 13th birthday. Gran is a real fairy godmother. She had tickets for the stage musical 'Wicked' which I'd always wanted to see. We had seats in the stalls near the front and I was rapt the whole way through. I was transported to a different place and time. "This is what I want to do," I thought to myself, "but I'll never be good enough."

I returned home late on Sunday evening on a high. Even the thoughts of the new phone failed to dampen my spirits. I didn't want to return home but knew I had to as there was school on Monday. I knew I wouldn't be able to share my joy with anyone. Mum wouldn't believe that I had enjoyed myself so much even if I tried to tell her. It just wasn't her idea of a birthday celebration. If I told the girls at school they would poke fun at me. Their idea of having fun wouldn't be fun unless boys were involved.

Mum did ask me about the weekend. I don't know why but I didn't want to sound too enthusiastic about it and played it down. It may have been because I had a feeling she may have been jealous that I could enjoy myself more with Gran than with her. I told her I thought the phone was 'fab'.

So many memories!

Amanda

20th May

Dear H,

Gran has just phoned to tell me she has spoken to
Holly Field, the singing teacher. Her proper title is 'Vocal
coach'. All I have to do is to phone her and make
a time for my first lesson. Gran told me that Mrs
Field used to be known by her stage name of Georgia
Mansfield. She was once a world famous vocalist but
she has now retired from full-time stage work and
prefers to teach instead. Gran said, "She sounds a
really nice lady. I'm sure you'll get on well with her."

I feel sick just thinking of it. Now that the time
has come, I don't know whether I can carry it
off. I suppose I haven't a choice as Gran has
gone to so much trouble. I can't let her down.
From a very 'uncertain' Amanda

26th May

Dear H,

I feel terrible. I just couldn't face phoning Holly Field. I kept putting it off. Eventually, Gran forced me. She told me she was really disappointed in me after she had gone to all of the trouble to find a teacher. I felt I'd let her down. Eventually I plucked up my courage. I didn't have a choice.

The lessons begin in three weeks' time. I feel as though I'm on a see-saw!

"Here we go again," I can hear you say.

Sometimes I'm up and sometimes I'm down.

Last night I had a terrifying dream. I was on stage all ready to sing. The music began and I tried to open my mouth to sing and I couldn't. My lips were stuck together. All the girls at school fell on the floor in fits of giggles. Cassandra was the worst and kept mimicking me. It was so embarrassing. I woke up with a racing heart and had to take several deep breaths to calm myself down.

At other times I feel fine and tell myself that I've as much right to have lessons as anyone else. What have I got to lose? I look into the future and ask myself, "How will I feel when I'm older if I don't give myself a chance?" I know the answer.

No one can do this for me. I've got to do it myself. If the worst thing happens and the teacher thinks I'm hopeless, I can stop the

lessons and no one will be any the wiser. The words

of a song appear from nowhere,

'There is love if you look

That will lift you up high.

Put your faith in the future,

Trust your feelings inside.'

I've GOT to give it a go!!!

Amanda

16th June

Dear H,

TODAY IS THE DAY! I'm tempted to phone Holly Field and say I'm ill. I REALLY, REALLY am. I feel so sick and I've got these huge butterflies doing somersaults in my tummy.

This is the plan. (That's if I go ahead with it.) The lesson begins at 4.15pm. I'm going to catch the school bus home as usual and call in at home to change. Then Gran suggested I ride my bike to the lesson so I'm not late. That will be a laugh!! I haven't ridden my bike for ages. It's so long ago I can't recall it. I hope I can remember HOW to ride!!

Keep your fingers crossed for me!

Well, I've done it! I went for my first singing lesson!

I feel quite proud of myself that I actually plucked

up my courage and went but not in other ways. I

don't know what Mrs Field thought of me. Because

I'd exerted myself riding my bike, I was boiling hot

when I arrived and I felt as though I needed a

shower.

As I told you, I hadn't ridden my bike for ages.

I found it really hard at first. I was so short of

breath. My balance was off-tilt and I was wobbling

all over the place and then it seemed as though

I was on auto pilot because it all came back to

me. The only problem was the muscles down the

front of my thighs!! They hurt so much and my

thigh muscles have been so sore ever since. I can

hardly walk up the stairs at home! Mum gave me

a puzzled frown and asked me if I was okay. I told

her I was stiff because we'd been practising jumps at school! I don't want her getting suspicious.

Well, I got a bit side-tracked there. I'm sure my face was the colour of beetroot when I arrived at Mrs Fields. I'd tied my hair back, but as usual, it was sticking out all over the place. I haven't got Gran's technique with it! When I walked up the drive towards the front door I could hear another student singing. My hands were sweaty and they started to shake. I was so nervous and scared. My mouth was dry and I was having problems swallowing. I wondered if I'd be able to talk, let alone sing.

Eventually, Mrs Field, the singing teacher, arrived at the door, and her previous student left. She was really friendly, asked me in and offered me a cold drink. We had a chat about the songs I'd like to sing. I mentioned some of the songs from my favourite CDs, and the two songs that I'd heard the girl in the wheel chair sing and guess what? Mrs Field told me that she taught another girl who sang those songs AND that she was in a wheel chair! Her name is Emma. I'd so like to meet her. She was the one who inspired me to do this. I doubt she'll ever realise.

Mrs Field had prepared an exercise disk for me. She told me I had to take it home with me and practise the exercises daily before I began to sing. She says it will help to warm my voice up. She told me the correct way to stand and how to breathe and then she asked me to sing the notes she was going to play on the piano. At first I felt as if my voice had disappeared into the tips of my toes. It just wasn't there. It felt thin and my throat was tight. I panicked.

Inside my head a voice was saying, "You can't sing. You can't sing. You shouldn't have come. Go home!"

It went on and on and I couldn't think straight. I felt a fool. I felt like running straight out of the room and never coming back. Cassandra's right. I am stupid.

Mrs Field told me not to worry and we did some breathing exercises which helped me to relax a bit. After a while I could feel my voice was returning but not to its normal strength. Mrs Field stopped playing the piano and looked at me. Immediately I thought, here goes, I'm no good BUT guess what? I can't believe it! She said, and I'll never forget it,

"Amanda, you have a beautiful voice but we need to do a lot of work on it. It will take time but we'll get there if you are prepared to put in the effort and trust me."

I felt like bursting into tears. "Oh, I'm prepared to put in the effort. I really want to try." I stammered bottling up my emotions.

"That's good. We really need you to relax and concentrate on your breathing. Practise with the disk at home and I'll look out for that music for you for next week," she said.

The lesson passed far too quickly and it was soon time for home. Part of me enjoyed it and another part didn't. I was annoyed with myself. I felt as though I could have sung better and that I didn't really show Mrs Field how well I can sing.

All the way home so many things were going on inside my head. Mrs Field told me I had a beautiful voice, that's fantastic, if she was speaking the truth. Why would she tell lies? She also said there's a long way to go. I'm not sure whether she's trying to be kind to me or put me off or what? Why do I always have so many doubts? I told Mrs Field that I'd try and I meant it. Now I feel like just giving up and never going back again.

Feeling in a muddle! Help!

Love, Amanda

17th June

Dear H,

Gran rang me as soon as I arrived home from the first lesson. I think she got the impression that something was not okay. She started to prod me and began asking me lots of searching questions. I hope I didn't sound ungrateful. I didn't mean to. Once I began, I just blabbed. I couldn't stop myself. It just all came out. I don't think she got a word in as I was talking so much.

I told her about how wretched I feel about myself and that if I don't do something well, then I feel hopeless at it. That makes me feel a failure.

I wanted to go to the singing lesson and sing how

I do at home when I'm on my own. I was just so nervous I couldn't stop shaking. It was better after I'd done the breathing exercises but by then I felt such an idiot. I don't know whether I can face going through it all again.

Gran is fantastic. She listened to everything I had to say. When I'd finished and after I'd had a howl, she talked me through the things that I had mentioned that were wrong in my life.

"Let's focus on one thing at a time shall we? You are looking at the whole picture and although there are lots of things you aren't happy about, we can't sort all of them out at once. How about taking the singing and dealing with that first? Let's work on one problem at a time shall we?"

"I don't think I can go back," I blurted.

"Okay, give it a few days to think about it. If after that, you are certain that you never want to sing again, I'll cancel the lessons, Let me know what you decide to do," said Gran.

I didn't feel very proud of myself so I snuck down to the pantry and grabbed a few boxes of snack biscuits and took refuge in my room. No need to tell you, I stuffed myself silly and then felt worse than ever.

I'm hopeless. Why do I put myself through all of this? It would be so much easier to forget the idea. It would be far less stressful. I feel,

'I need time

To sort out myself,

To find out

What life is all about.

I'm travelling in a circle

And getting nowhere fast.'

It's much easier to jot my feelings down like this

than to explain them to anyone, except for you of

course.

From an 'unsure' Amanda

20th June

Dear H,

I've had three days to think about what Gran said. I know I over-reacted. I was really silly. I've got to try to cope better. I've worked it out that I can't be perfect from the start otherwise why would I need to have lessons.

Ever since I calmed down, I've been practising my singing exercises everyday. I'm still not ever so confident but I'm trying. I stand in front of the mirror in my bedroom to make sure my posture is correct and I'm opening my mouth wide enough. I'm learning paradoxical breathing. Mrs Field explained to me how this opens up the rib cage, and because there is more air, the voice is stronger. As you breathe in, you pull your tummy muscles in, and as you breathe out, you relax your tummy muscles. It takes a bit of practice, but I'm getting there. I'm going to practise my songs now.

I'm beginning to look forward to the next lesson.

Give me strength!

Amanda!

23rd June

Dear H,

Gran was really thrilled and relieved to hear that I'd decided to give the singing lessons another go. I've just returned from my second lesson and although I was still nervous I didn't feel as scared as I did the first time I went.

When I arrived, Mrs Field said she had a surprise waiting for me! I couldn't believe my eyes when I walked into the music room. There was Emma, the girl in the wheelchair! She had a big grin on her face and I immediately felt as though I'd known her for ever. Mrs Field suggested that we share our singing lessons for a few weeks. It was a welcome relief. I could sing with Emma and it wouldn't matter so much if I messed up as I wouldn't be singing all alone. We began with the exercises on the disk which would help us to loosen our voices and stop us straining them.

Emma had brought in backing CDs of the songs that she had sung at the concert and which I had liked so much. She said I could borrow them and that we could try singing them together.

I really enjoyed singing with Emma. But I never realised that singing was so complicated. There are so many things to think about all at once. You have to stand correctly and remember the paradoxical breathing at the same time as sounding the words correctly. It's really tricky.

I'm going to practise and practise until I get everything right.

La,

La,   La,

La,   La,

La,   La,

La,   La!!!!!

It's strange, but when I told Gran that Emma had been at my singing lesson, she didn't seem surprised. Hmm, I'm wondering if Gran has a sneaky side to her personality!! I don't really mind. Sharing the lessons with Emma has certainly helped to build my confidence.

Feeling great!

Amanda

22nd July

Dear H,

Life has been so full on; I haven't had time to write lately.

I've been so busy with homework and practising my singing. I've been going to Mrs Field's now for six weeks. Mrs Field suggested that I now return to having a private singing lesson. I will miss Emma but we speak quite often on the phone now. My new mobile is coming in useful after all. Emma doesn't live too far away from me so I can still see her. In a way I'm pleased as I can concentrate on singing the songs I want to sing.

Mrs Field is helping me to choose songs that

are suited to my voice. I'm experimenting with different styles: pop, jazz, blues, songs from musicals, everything. I love to sing everything except opera. Mrs. Field says that I'm a soprano but I have a good range so I can also sing songs with lower notes. Mrs. Field is strict but very kind. She is quite happy for me to choose my songs but I have to sing them properly and she's a stickler for getting everything correct. She says, "I must be able to hear every word you are singing Amanda and sing the words as though you mean them."

We are preparing a disk of my singing which I'm going to send to Gran as a surprise!

Mrs Field seems amazed at how fast I'm improving. She said she wished all her students would work as

hard as me. I don't call this work. I absolutely love
to practice!!

Talk to you soon, I promise,

Amanda

27th July

Dear H,

School drags on the same. 'Queen' Cassandra still rules supremely in her court closely surrounded at all times by her ladies in waiting! She has really got the girls in her clique under her thumb. They are so tightly knit that I don't think they could escape even if they chose to do so. I think I told you they have special seats on the school bus and she won't allow them to sit anywhere else. All members of the clique have to promise that they'll follow her set of rules. If they don't, she told them she'll make sure their lives won't be worth living. She is a first class bully. I can't understand it. The girls in the clique aren't stupid. Some of them are very bright. They sit in THEIR seats on the bus making fun of everyone. They sure must have big problems! I thought I was the one with ALL the problems but I'm beginning to wonder.

It was my turn today. As I was stepping off the bus from school I heard Cassandra whispering, "What's happened to Piggy? She's walking around with a glazed expression on her face. I wonder if she has a boyfriend."

One of her buddies said loudly, "He must be desperate to go out with her!!"

Of course, everyone laughed. They hardly ever have the courage to say such things to your face.

Cassandra still upsets me but I think I'm beginning to learn how to deal with her. I don't feel as though she is undermining me as she used to and I'm feeling more in control of my emotions. If she knows she's upset someone, she'll torment them worse than ever. The trick is trying to ignore her and the rest of them. It's not easy.

Emma told me that she suffered an awful lot after she returned to school after her accident. She was the only student there in a wheelchair. Most kids were really sympathetic but another clique at Emma's school followed her around for weeks and made her life unbearable. I don't understand how people can be so cruel. Emma suggested I try to ignore them and it has helped. She said that eventually they will get fed up and start on someone else.

It's good to have a real person of a similar age to confide in.

From a 'more in control'

Amanda

14th August

Dear H,

You won't believe it! I actually plucked up the courage to audition for the school choir! And I was accepted! When I sang, Mr Brookes, the music teacher said, "I never knew you could sing like that, Amanda!"

I thought to myself, "There's a lot about me you don't know."

Some of the other choir members must have heard my audition and stared at me in astonishment. Mr Brookes must have made a comment to one of the other teachers who said, "I've heard you have a lovely singing voice Amanda."

My self-esteem suddenly rocketed.

It's odd, but whenever I walk into a classroom, and everyone is talking, they all seem to stop and stare at me. Perhaps it's my imagination, but I thought I heard someone mention something about my voice.

Isn't it strange that when you have something that other people admire they do one of two things? They either cling around you as if they are hoping to catch it from you or they make snide comments and pretend it's the last thing on earth they would like to have. Interesting isn't it?

Have you ever noticed that?

Amanda

15th September

Dear H,

Do you know? I've just realised that no one has called me Piggy for weeks. Unfortunately, Cassandra has to stand behind me at choir practice because she's taller than I am. She keeps referring to me sarcastically as THE DIVA. At least, it's better than Piggy!!

From THE DIVA!! Ha, Ha!!!

20th September

Dear H,

It's hard to believe but I've lost a lot of weight and my clothes are hanging off me. I have to put a safety pin in the waistband of my school skirt, otherwise it would fall down.

Mum came knocking on my door last night. She seemed quite embarrassed. She said, "It's such a long time since we've had a 'heart to heart' talk. I'm really pleased that you seem happier. I know I'm always so busy and I wanted to apologise for leaving you on your own so much. I think we should go on a shopping spree. What do you think? You could certainly do with some new clothes. You've lost a lot of weight. You're growing up so quickly!"

I was so surprised. Mum really did seem enthusiastic about spending some time with me. I have suspicions that Gran may have whispered in her ear.

Your 'surprised' friend,

Amanda

26th September

Dear H,

I've been looking in the mirror. Remember how I hated to do that?

I've grown taller, and it's true that I have lost weight. I'm not what you would call slim. I can't ever imagine myself as being petite but I'm now much happier with the way I am. It just wouldn't suit me to be skinny. I've noticed my muscles are more toned and I don't appear to be quite such a frump as I once did. It must be all the bike riding I'm doing. I have more energy now and I finally have some colour in my cheeks. I can actually look at myself and I don't hate what I see.

Another thought has crossed my mind. I've realised I don't eat as much junk food either. I'm so keen to practise my singing when I arrive home, that I become totally absorbed in practising all the songs I know. Usually I forget to eat anything until dinner.

Do you know? I no longer have the constant desire to stuff myself with food. Isn't that fantastic? I'm not Miss Perfect though. I do still get the urge to eat chocolate when something drastic happens, but thankfully, that isn't as frequent as it used to be.

Mum still doesn't know about the singing lessons because I always make sure I clear my music and CDs away before she arrives home. One of these days she's going to arrive home 'out of the blue' and the secret will be out.

I'd love to talk to Mum and Dad about the singing. I do feel very sneaky and worry a bit about how it's all going to sort itself out. We haven't really talked for so long about personal stuff; you know about what's been happening at school with Cassandra. I don't feel able to confide in them. It's okay to talk about everyday topics, but when it comes to talking about the things that are really important to me, it's a different matter. I would love to share more of myself with them. I sometimes feel as though they really don't know ME at all. It would be awesome if I could talk about my love of singing and about all the things I write to you about. I wish I could talk to Mum and Dad like I do with Gran. In general, things are getting better but there's still a way to go.

Sometimes, I feel so grown up and at other times, I feel like a little girl. I desperately crave for my parents' acknowledgement that I'm doing okay and that I'm accepted. I need their understanding. I need their support and love. But at the same time, I do need to be my own person. Perhaps if we could break down the barriers more they would see that I'm not a little kid anymore.

Yours,

Amanda

30th September

Dear H,

I'VE HAD THE MOST MARVELLOUS DAY EVER!

Mum, true to her word, suggested that we go on a shopping spree. I will admit I was really looking forward to choosing some new clothes. A few months ago I would have probably made lots of excuses not to go. I would have felt so embarrassed trying to squeeze into clothes that were too small.

I'd been looking at what other girls of my age were wearing and flicking through some teen magazines that Mum had left around, (now I come to think of it, probably on purpose). I was really keen to get started and Mum seemed as excited as I did. We left straight after breakfast. Mum looked exquisite as she always does. I looked my normal frumpy self. In fact, I must have looked downright daggy as the only clothes I had to wear were far too big for me.

Mum's VERY organised and had made a list of boutiques who stocked designer clothes for my age. I was a bit in awe when she began. I hoped that the clothes she had in mind were similar to the ones I'd seen in the magazines. I need not have worried! It was wonderful to be able to enter a shop and find clothes that fitted me and looked good on my size. I tried on just about everything; jeans, tops, jackets, accessories. There was just so much!

Mum tried to influence me on a few occasions so our 'Mum-daughter bonding day' was not without a few hassles but, listening to the conversations of the girls on the bus from school, I get the impression they all have the odd disagreements over clothes with their Mums.

Mum went overboard and spent and spent. She even suggested she treat me to new sets of underwear and shoes! I didn't complain. I really did need some new bras as the ones I was wearing were completely the wrong size. I think Mum felt guilty for ignoring me for so long.

I don't want to sound big headed but I was amazed at how good I looked in the mirror. I didn't want to wear my old clothes again and left the boutique wearing one of my new outfits.

Mum suggested we take a break for lunch and hurried me, and lots of bags and packages, into a new French Bistro she had heard of. After we had ordered she said, "I've made an appointment at the hair stylist's. You will come, won't you?"

I thought the appointment was just for her but when we arrived I found out that it was for both of us. Mum said, "We've got to complete the new image. I'm treating you to a restyle."

I was speechless. It was like winning a competition. Suddenly everything I'd always dreamed of was coming true. I wanted to give Mum a hug but I didn't feel I could go that far yet.

Mum had booked her own stylist, Philippe, to restyle my hair. He had won lots of awards for his styles and had a display of all his trophies in a prominent position on the wall so people could see them as they walked passed the salon.

Because my hair had always stuck out in the wrong places, Philippe suggested a short style, which he said was very popular, easy to manage and would suit my face shape. No more straightening lotions! I nearly had a fit as he began to cut my hair and I could see great chunks on the floor. I thought I'd have no hair left, but I shouldn't have worried. When he'd finished and shown me how to blow dry my hair, I was ecstatic. It was so easy. All I had to do was to use some styling gel and run my fingers through my hair as I dried it. Wow! And Wow again!

When I looked in the mirror, I couldn't believe it. The face that was staring back at me appeared to have hazel eyes where I had always thought them to be a dark, dingy brown and my copper hair was glinting. My freckles didn't seem so prominent, and I could see my cheek bones. Dare I say it? The shape of the face in the mirror reminded me a little of my Mum's.

You'll think I'm terribly spoilt! I had THE MOST WONDERFUL DAY! When we returned home Mum said, "Doesn't our daughter look fabulous?"

Dad was clearly taken aback and said he didn't recognise me. To put the 'icing on the cake,' Dad suggested that, as he had some time to spare, he would take his 'two gorgeous girls' out to dinner that evening.

As I walked out of the room to change into one

of my new outfits for dinner, I heard Dad ask Mum if she knew what had brought about this change in me. I heard Mum say, "I haven't the faintest idea. It may just be due to her growing up. All I can say is thank goodness. I was beginning to get really worried about her. At one stage I thought I'd have to book her in to see a cosmetic surgeon!"

Dad just grunted and replied, "I've never been able to understand women."

I'm relieved that our family is regaining some sort of normality although I was upset by Mum's comment.

I still don't fully understand myself. I'll never have a skinny model-like figure, but who cares! I'm beginning to feel more content with myself and how I look and that's what's important.

From a 'thankful' Amanda

2nd October

Dear H,

I'm gradually becoming used to my new appearance.
You should have seen the looks on the faces of the
girls at school! Cassandra looked as if she'd seen a
ghost! She stood there speechless with her mouth
wide open, and then rushed off to spread the news!

I must admit, I felt nervous going into school this
morning. I knew my changed appearance would cause
a stir. Quite a few of the girls and teachers told me
I looked good. I must admit, I'm feeling a lot better
about myself. I have more confidence and I feel I'm
accepted more, although I'll never be Miss Popularity!

I wonder if butterflies have feelings? Amanda

4th October

Dear H,

I've just returned from my singing lesson. Mrs Field was blown away with my new look. You should have seen the surprised expression on her face when she opened the door. She was almost as thrilled as I am with my make-over.

She also had some exciting news, except there's a problem. Mrs Field wants me to enter a musical competition. There's an annual event held in the city. It's really important. The official judges are all professional singers and voice coaches. If the judges feel that there is an exceptionally gifted singer, they offer one scholarship a year which entitles the winner to attend a prestigious music college called St Celia's Academy of Music for Talented and Gifted Students. That's a bit of a mouthful so, Mrs Field told me it's usually referred to as St C's. It has a fantastic reputation and it is a great honour to be invited to attend the School. Along with the normal school subjects you receive specialised training in your area of music. Mrs Field feels I'm ready to 'launch myself,' as she puts it.

The problem is that because I'm under 18, I need the signature of one of my parents before I can enter. There's another problem and that is the school isn't in our city which means I would have to board there and only come home in the holidays. There are quite a few important things to consider and I just hope something can be worked out. The concert is a really big occasion.

All the singers have to perform on stage at a theatre in the city. The girls all have sparkly stage outfits and have their hair and make-up done professionally.

The competition is in six weeks' time. I've chosen my songs just in case I'm allowed to enter. Mrs Field has even arranged for a dance teacher to give me some lessons to improve my stage presence, which just means helping me to move confidently on stage while I'm singing.

It's all very exciting. When I first began writing to you, I never thought my life would turn out like this. I want to enter the competition but I still feel scared. Will I ever stop feeling like this? I'll have to give Emma a phone call. She always makes me feel much calmer. I suppose her life is so much 'slower' in general and she looks at life from a completely different angle since her accident.

Mrs Field has spoken on the phone to Gran and they are trying to sort something out. Please keep your fingers crossed for me. I want to enter so much.

The sky's the limit!

Amanda

15th October

Dear H,

I can't believe it!! After all the secrecy!

The only way Gran could think of getting Mum to give permission for me to enter the competition was to tell her all about the singing lessons!! Gran explained it to her by saying that I had wanted to give Mum a surprise.

Gran did discuss it with me first. I wasn't keen on the idea but Gran said she couldn't think of anything else. She warned me that Mum might react in some way, especially as Gran had mentioned I would have to leave home during term time.

I'm finding all of this very strange. I could understand it if Mum had been angry or surprised but she took the news so calmly and it's worrying me. She's even suggested she'll take me to choose an outfit to wear at the concert and has booked me in to have my hair and stage make-up done.

I feel that something is weird - not quite right.

From a 'wondering' Amanda

16th November

Dear H,

Well, the concert is tomorrow evening!

We have rehearsals at the theatre in the morning and I'm off to the hairdressers and the beautician's tomorrow afternoon so I certainly won't have any spare time to write!!

Mum said I could choose anything I wanted to wear so I chose a sequined top with spaghetti straps. The colour is sea green and I have a matching swirly skirt.

The butterflies have been doing somersaults all day. Help! If I feel like this today, what am I going to feel like tomorrow? At the moment they are all performing wearing spiky boots!! I'm so nervous. I've hardly eaten all week, which is probably a good thing, because I've lost more weight.

Mum will drop me off at the theatre tomorrow evening. She says she'll try to be at the performance but she has someone important she has to pick up at the airport tomorrow. It's all very hush, hush. She doesn't appear to be that interested in coming to hear me sing. I suppose I am a bit disappointed that she's not interested but, on second thoughts, I may feel more comfortable singing knowing she isn't there. Part of me would really like her to be there though.

Keep your fingers crossed for me.
From your best friend, Amanda

18th November

Dear H,

I've got so much to tell you!!!

I stood backstage and listened to Emma singing her song. As I stood listening to her, my mind wandered back to the first time I had heard her sing. What an emotional wreck I was then! Life has certainly changed for me, and definitely for the better. For a moment, I became emotional and thought I was going to burst into tears, not because I was unhappy, but because life is now so much better and I feel so much happier. I stopped myself, just in time. I didn't want to ruin my eye makeup, especially since it had taken so long to put on.

For a second, the feelings of doubt returned, but I told myself that if Emma could do it, so could I. I talked myself through it, took some deep breaths and managed to calm myself. Emma was sitting in her wheelchair behind the curtains. She clasped my hand as I passed her. Just knowing she was close at hand gave me the courage I needed. I walked onto the stage, the curtains swished open and I DID IT!!! I began to sing, thinking only of what the words meant. I forgot all about my nerves and gave it all I had. WHAT A FANTASTIC FEELING! The audience clapped and cheered and even Mrs Field who had been backstage with me had tears in her eyes.

I then got a big surprise, because when all the competitors had finished performing and we were allowed to go to sit in the audience to await the judges' decision, I arrived with Mrs Field to sit down, and there was Mum, Dad and Gran sitting alongside my seat!! Gran was the important person Mum had been to collect at the airport. Mum had kept it a secret. They had ALL been at the concert and had heard me sing!!! I was blown away! There wasn't time to speak to them, because just then the chief judge was walking onto the stage, but I was ecstatic. I felt as if I could have hugged every one in the theatre! It was unreal.

The competition was divided into sections and I was thrilled when Emma won the prize in her section. When it came to the announcement of the winner for my section, I sat on the edge of my seat, clasped my hands together so tightly and closed my eyes. The butterflies in my tummy had returned wearing boxing gloves. My heart missed a beat as the winner was announced. I couldn't believe it. It wasn't me. I clapped really hard for the winner but felt as though I wanted to disappear through a hole in the floor. I was so disappointed. Perhaps I had imagined I was better than I thought I was. I felt like crying but bit my bottom lip as hard as I could to stop myself.   I was so lost in my thoughts that I wasn't listening to what was being said on the stage. Then, I realised they were going to announce the winner of the coveted prize, the scholarship to St C's. I didn't think I had a chance of winning.

The next thing I knew was that my family were jumping up and down, Gran had tears streaming down her face and my Mum had grasped me in a tight bear hug. Before I knew what was happening, I had been ushered up onto the stage in front of an applauding audience. No need to tell you. I HAD WON!!

Who would have thought it? It was a dream come true. Only a year ago, I was a plain, frumpy overweight girl who was so depressed and lonely. Now, I am looking towards the future with excitement and I am so positive that everything will work out for the best. I had thought life was not worth living and NOW I have EVERYTHING to live for.

WHOOPPEE!

   WHOOPPEE!!

      WHOOPPEE!!!

I'm so happy, I could sing from the roof tops!!

From a 'terrifically excited' Amanda

19th November

Dear H,

As soon as I could, I phoned Mrs Field for a catch-up. As you can imagine, she was ecstatic. She suggested, "How about us having a celebration dinner together before you go away?"

I answered, "Yes, that would be lovely but I would enjoy it so much more if Emma could come too."

"What a wonderful idea! I'm sure we can arrange it."

Mrs Field, true to her word, contacted Emma and not long after, we met at a lovely restaurant for dinner. When we had finished our meal I told Emma

I had a secret that I wanted to share with her.
She looked astonished when I told her that she had
been my inspiration and that if I had not heard
her sing that afternoon at the school concert, I
would have never had the courage to take my life in
my hands to try to change things for the better.
She was astounded and at first couldn't speak. Her
eyes glistened with tears and she enveloped me in
her arms. She had shared her story with me before
about how she had been left severely disabled, but
one thing she could still do was to sing. She said it
was something she loved to do and was thrilled that
she had helped me. She said, "Before you go, I've got
a little surprise for you."

I look at her in astonishment. I didn't expect
anything from her. Her gift of friendship was
enough. She presented me with a small gift

wrapped box. She said, "I'd like you to open it now, go on."

I had no idea what the box contained, but I was thrilled when I opened it to see what it contained, a silver pendant and chain. When I looked closely, I could see that it was similar to the one Emma was wearing. The pendant was in the shape of a daisy with my birthstone, set into one of the petals. Emma explained to me that the name 'daisy' had many meanings. One of her favourites was the astrological meaning of 'quiet strength'. She said it reminded her of me, but more important than that was that the daisy represented the 'Daisy Chain.'

Emma explained that she had recently read about the 'Daisy Chain' in a magazine and had instantly thought of me. She told me the idea had been started by someone similar to me, who had experienced bullying whilst she was at school. She's now in her twenties, but she had remembered picking daisies when she had been younger. She had made them into daisy chains by making a slit in the stem of each daisy and threading the stem of another daisy to make a chain which she then made into a necklace.

The symbolism behind this idea is that if we join the daisies together into a 'chain' we can combat bullying. By wearing the daisy, people will know that you are part of a network that promotes and supports anti-bullying and that they can go to you for help and that you will be able to empathise with them and offer support. Emma told me that the idea was spreading and a lot of schools had 'Daisy Chains.'

As some schools forbid their students from wearing jewellery at school, there was a special card, in the shape of a daisy, which you could give to people to let them know you were anti-bullying. In this way, you could approach other students without anyone else knowing.

 I thought it was a terrific idea and wished we'd had a 'Daisy Chain' at St Ursula's. If I ever think that someone is being bullied, I will introduce the idea to them.

I feel Emma and I will always have a special bond and we will continue to be the best of friends forever.

From your 'emotional' friend,
Mandy

PS

I forgot to tell you my other exciting news. There was a young and over enthusiastic reporter from the local newspaper at the concert. When I was declared the winner of the scholarship, he asked my parents if I could be featured in the newspaper. They agreed, so my photo was splashed across the front page with the heading, 'AMANDA, SUPER STAR!' You can imagine the result, the news spread around the school like 'wild fire'.

All of a sudden, I appeared to be THE most important person in the whole school. Everyone seemed to want to know me and become my best friend. That is, all except for Cassandra who completely ignored me. She walked around with her nose stuck in the air.

As a result, I was asked to perform at the last assembly of the term before school finished for the Christmas holidays. I sang the same songs that I had performed at the concert. I was so proud that Mum took some time off work to come and listen to me. It made all the difference in more ways than one, but I'll tell you about it tomorrow.

5th December

Dear H,

I decided to wear my daisy pendant at the
performance. Another parent, attending the
assembly, commented on it and asked me if it
was one of the anti-bullying Daisy Chain pendants.
When I replied that it was, she enquired where she
could purchase one for a young relative who was
being bullied. Mum looked a bit uneasy. The parent
continued to praise the idea behind the Daisy
Chain while Mum appeared to become even more
unnerved.

When I arrived home from school, Mum surprisingly
was home and brought up the subject of the
significance of the pendant. She suggested we go

into the kitchen and have a drink. It appeared
the comments made by the parent had made her
inquisitive and had led to her doing some research
that afternoon on the internet. She had read the
story from the magazine that Emma had told me
about. She was aware that the pendant had been
a gift from Emma but not why she'd chosen to
give me a Daisy Chain pendant.

I became very uncomfortable, began to fidget and
felt myself blushing. She told me that Gran had
hinted to her on a few occasions over the last
few months that it was about time she sat and
had a good chat with me. She hadn't mentioned
what is was all about as she said it wasn't her
place to do so. Mum and I have become much
closer but still weren't in the habit of discussing
personal issues. Mum hadn't known how to begin

the conversation. She still was unsure what the problem was so had shied away from approaching me. She said she'd wanted to on numerous occasions but hadn't known how to begin, that was until today when the comments from the parent had made things so much clearer.

A few months ago, I wouldn't have felt confident enough to have had this conversation. I would have most likely told Mum everything was fine, but now, I'm different, more in charge of myself. I thought, 'It's now or never,' and came out with the whole Cassandra saga. Mum sat 'gob-smacked' while I related the whole sorry story.

'But why didn't you tell me?' she eventually managed to ask.

"I just couldn't. You wouldn't have understood. You thought the sun shone out of Cassandra. You wouldn't have believed me."

This opened the 'flood gates'. Both of us had tears rolling down our cheeks. There were lots of sopping wet tissues and two blotchy red faces. It was the kind of talk we should have been having on a regular basis and it ended with the biggest HUG! Better late than never!

From a 'much relieved and emotionally drained' Amanda

20th December

Dear H,

I'm so thrilled, delighted etc. Mum and Dad are taking a month's leave from work over Christmas so that we can spend time together as a family before I go away to St C's in the New Year. It's amazing what changes can take place in the space of a year and a half.

Mum felt so guilty about her lack of understanding over the past. Since the 'serious chat' and consequent melt down, we now have a closer bond but there's still a way to go, but I'm not complaining. We have the rest of our lives to catch up. Obviously, Mum shared some of the 'chat' with Dad. As a consequence, my relationship with both of my parents has improved tremendously. They are so proud of my achievements and say they will support me all the way.

Mum has also confided in me about another incident which had happened before the competition and had left her feeling isolated and had sent her on a walk of reflection. She told me how, a few weeks ago, one of her wealthy clients had congratulated her on having a daughter with such a marvellous singing voice. Obviously, Mum had been surprised by this news, but had not let on she didn't know what the woman was talking about. Mum told me she had been livid with me and had felt like rushing home and confronting me. She had wanted to know all about the singing lessons, had wondered who had paid for them and especially the reason I had kept it such a secret.

She told me how instead of rushing to confront me, she had driven from work in a huff to Haddon Park where she had walked round and round the lake until she cooled down. She had remembered an argument that she had had with her mother, my Gran, when she had been a similar age to me. The result of that had been that she and her mother had not spoken for days. The rift had never really been healed. It appears Mum could be quite stubborn when she was my age and all she and Gran did was to disagree about everything.

And what had the argument been all about? Mum had annoyed Gran because Mum wouldn't listen to what she was saying! She always thought she knew better than Gran. Mum said she had had a good think, and then had realised how little she had actually listened to me.

Mum told me that she had felt so terribly guilty and had felt that she was a rotten Mum who was so carried away with her own ambitions that she hardly had any time to spend with me.

She then went on to tell me that Gran had phoned her to discuss the singing competition and had mentioned that the singing was a surprise for her. That news made her feel less upset. Mum has admitted a lot to me, that she had forgotten what it was like to be young and to feel insecure. I am grateful for her honesty.

Love from a 'grateful'

Amanda

7th January

Dear H,

Well, after a super Christmas and a brilliant New Year celebration, there's a lot of stuff I need to do before I begin my new school life at St C's. I have to buy books etc. for my 'normal' lessons and I have to order my new school uniform, blue this time, which is not nearly as formal and hideous as I had to wear at the last place! I'll be very busy.

As I mentioned before, the school is too far away for me to commute daily, I'll have to board there during term time and will fly home every school holiday. It's rather scary when I think about it. I've been sent lots of information about the school. The majority of the students are boarders and we each have our own room containing bed, wardrobe, study desk and bathroom. I will be in Grantham House where all the girls board. There are House Mothers there, some of who teach part-time but their main task is to be there for the boarders. They arrange activities for us at weekends and make sure we are OK. I'm lucky, as the school isn't too far away from Gran's house, so some weekends, I can go to stay with her. That will be great and something to look forward to.

Can't wait!

Amanda

27th January

Dear H,

At last, I'm packed and all ready to go. Mum and Dad are flying to St C's with me as there is a special afternoon tea and tour of the school to welcome all new students and their parents. Mum and Dad are also interested to see where I'll be studying for the next few years and they also want to meet with some of the teachers and parents of the other students.

I'm looking forward to meeting new friends who will have music as their main interest. At least, I'll have something in common with them, not like at my old school! Mum and Dad are going to stay close by in a hotel for a few days, just to make sure I'm okay as it's the first time I've been away from home for any length of time. They've promised they'll only call in to see me if I ask them to. I don't want the other students to think I can't look after myself. I feel quite touched in a way as at least it means they care about me. But I'll be back at Easter for the holiday. I'm thrilled that I no longer have to go to St Ursula's. There is one person there who I especially won't miss!

I've grown up a lot since I first began writing to you and have experienced a rollercoaster of emotions. I now know my parents better and am beginning to see things from their point of view. I don't think I'll ever reach the stage where Mum are I will be best buddies all the time but we are so much closer than we've ever been.

I'm eternally grateful to my Gran for believing in me and being so supportive. It's a relief that Mum has begun to heal the rift she's had for so long with Gran. Again, I don't ever think it's going to be the easiest of relationships, but it's improving.

I owe heaps to Mrs. Field. If it had not been for her I wouldn't be where I am now. When I felt so insecure and hopeless she was always there encouraging me and always helping me to believe in myself. She could sense my insecurities, and I now know she invited Emma to share my singing lessons on purpose so that I could concentrate on my singing and not think so much about how I was feeling.

I am eternally thankful for Emma, who unknowingly inspired me to do bigger and better things. She's the best friend I always wanted. I can talk to her about anything. She appears much older than her 15 years and she has the ability to understand me probably more than I understand myself.

Then there's you. What would I have done without you? You know me inside out. You are my conscience, my other half. Writing to you, H, has kept me on the straight and narrow. I would have gone crazy without you.

Of course, I'm not expecting the rest of my life to be trouble free. I'm not that stupid. I still have anxieties and I think I always will have. The difference now is that I realise I have so much to be thankful for. There are so many people supporting me. I know I'm not alone and that if, and when, I have problems, there are people out there who love me and will be there for me.

I'm not going to let anyone down, ESPECIALLY MYSELF!

A 'massive thanks' to everyone,

Love you all!

Amanda

FABULOUS SUPERSTAR!

'I'm forever reaching

For a shooting star.

Music in my soul,

Music in my heart,

Cascading rhythms

Are tearing me apart.

Fabulous superstar!

Name up in lights,

Couldn't happen to me.

Excuses are mine,

It's the wrong place,

It's the wrong time.

I am the sun, the star

Ready to shine.

I must stretch, reach out

Aim high as the sky.

Better to fail

Than never to try.

I have travelled this far,

No more regrets.

Lived for this moment,

Nobody to blame,

Sense the fear

And taste the fame.'

To Dennis
for his constant encouragement.

Thank you to Tika and Kate
for your belief in the publication of this book.
Here it is at last!

ISBN 978-0-646-92550-9

© M Diane Guntrip, 2014

www.dianeguntrip.com

Layout and design by All In One Book Design (www.allinonebookdesign.com.au)
Printed by Optima Press, Western Australia

15179821R00104

Printed in Great Britain
by Amazon.co.uk, Ltd.,
Marston Gate.